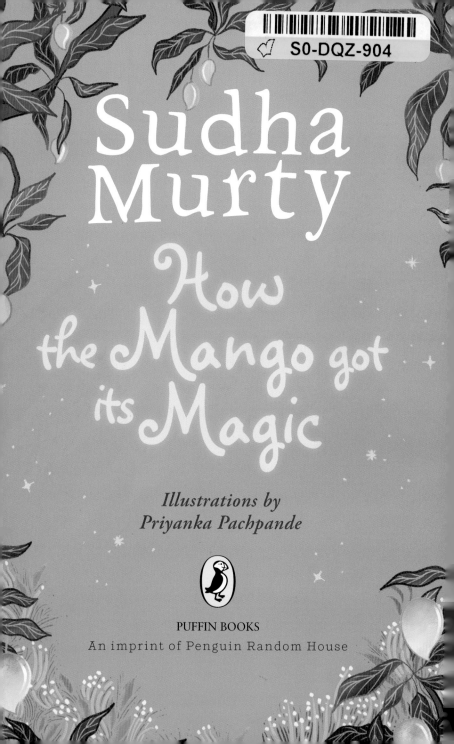

Sudha Murty

How the Mango got its Magic

Illustrations by
Priyanka Pachpande

PUFFIN BOOKS
An imprint of Penguin Random House

PUFFIN BOOKS

USA | Canada | UK | Ireland | Australia
New Zealand | India | South Africa | China

Puffin Books is part of the Penguin Random House group of companies
whose addresses can be found at global.penguinrandomhouse.com

Published by Penguin Random House India Pvt. Ltd
4th Floor, Capital Tower 1, MG Road,
Gurugram 122 002, Haryana, India

Penguin
Random House
India

First published in Puffin Books by Penguin Random House India 2022

ISBN 9780143447078

Typeset in Cormorant
Book design and layout by Canato Jimo
Printed at Aarvee Promotions, India

www.penguin.co.in

*Dedicated to all the people around
the world who love mangoes.
May you always enjoy the magic
of its sweetness...*

Chapter One

Once upon a time, there was a beautiful mango grove on the outskirts of a village. Dinkar was the owner of the grove and Shyam was his hardworking son.

Back in those days, mangoes were ornamental fruits with beautiful colours and shapes, but they were not very tasty—they were more sour than sweet.

When Dinkar opened the door, he saw an old man standing at his doorstep. The old man said, 'Hello. I got caught in the rain. Will you let me in? I will leave once it stops raining.'

Dinkar generously welcomed him in. 'It looks like the rain will not stop today, but it may cease tomorrow. Please come in. You can take shelter here.'

SCUTTLE! SCUTTLE!

One day, it
began to rain heavily
and there was a knock on
the door of Dinkar's house.

KNOCK KNOCK KNOCK

2

The old man entered the house. Shyam made him a hot meal and gave him some water to drink. The old man gulped the water down and devoured the food quickly, within minutes.

After a loud burp of satisfaction, he smiled at Shyam and Dinkar and said, 'That was a wholesome meal.'

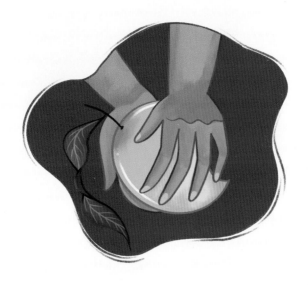

He took out a mango from his bag and gave it to Dinkar. 'This is for both of you,' he said. 'Please cut it and eat it immediately.'

Dinkar looked at the mango. It looked like it was one of the very sour ones. He did not want to insult his guest, so he cut the mango and bit into it. His eyes popped in wonder and he turned to his son, 'Shyam, all the mangoes I have eaten in my life have been sour—like the taste of lemon. Though we have a mango grove, we never eat the mangoes that grow here. But this mango is fantastic and unusually sweet. It's absolutely delicious! Go on, try it.'

Shyam took his first bite and nodded his head vigorously in agreement. This mango was indeed sweet and tasty. Shyam had never even heard of sweet mangoes!

'Plant this mango seed. The tree will grow quickly and produce more mangoes like the one you ate just now,' the old man smiled and said.

The next morning it stopped raining. The old man thanked Dinkar and Shyam for their timely hospitality and left.

Chapter Two

Immediately after the old man went on his way, Shyam ran to the mango grove and carefully planted the precious seed.

The tree grew very quickly, just like the old man had said, and in no time it began to flower. Within a few months, golden mangoes were hanging from the branches.

Shyam went to the grove every day to check on them. He enjoyed watching the fruits grow and ripen.

One day, he decided that
it was time to pluck the ripe
mangoes. He marked the mangoes on
one branch of the tree for ease and decided
to bring a basket the next day to collect them.

The following day to his astonishment, the
marked mangoes had vanished! There were
mangoes in all the other trees in the grove but
not on the one branch that he had marked on the
special tree!

'Someone has stolen my chosen mangoes,'
he thought, disappointed.

Shyam called the caretaker of the grove and instructed him, 'Please keep an eye on this specific tree, as the mangoes here are special and precious. I have marked another set of mangoes on the tree. They will be ready to be plucked by next week. I will come and collect them.'

Convinced that his mangoes were now safe, he went home.

The next week, Shyam went to harvest the mangoes. 'Oh no, not again! The mangoes that I had marked are not there on the branch!' Indeed, there were mangoes in all the other trees in the grove but not the ones that he had marked on the special tree!

He was distraught. He questioned the caretaker, 'Did you take the mangoes from this tree?'

The caretaker was offended. 'Sir, you appointed me to keep an eye on the mangoes. Then why would I steal them? Besides, if I wanted the mangoes, I could have asked you directly because you would have given them to me.

'I have done my duty, sir, and the truth is that I have not seen anyone enter or leave the mango grove without my knowledge. I was here every day from seven in the morning to seven at night, throughout the week. I can assure you that the mangoes were there yesterday during my shift.'

Shyam was perplexed. 'Perhaps the intruder comes at night,' he thought. 'In that case, I should appoint a security guard for the night.'

The new security guard was appointed for night duty, and he received the same instructions, 'Please keep an eye on this specific tree, as the mangoes here are special and precious. By next week, the mangoes on this marked branch will be ready to be plucked and I will come to collect them. I don't want these mangoes stolen at any cost. I will hold you responsible if something happens to them.'

The night guard nodded. 'Don't worry, sir. I will take care of the tree,' he said.

The next week, Shyam went to gather the mangoes. To his amazement, the marked mangoes were not there on the branch, yet again! There were mangoes in all the other trees in the grove, but not on the branch he had marked on the special tree! Again!

He called the night security guard, 'Do you sleep at night during your shift?' he asked furiously.

'No, sir, I was awake all night.'

'Then where are the mangoes?'

The night guard replied, 'Sir, I was guarding the tree all night and the mangoes were most definitely there. In the wee hours of the morning, I smelled a wonderful aroma. I looked around for a quick check but could not figure out where it was coming from. So, I returned to my station, completed my shift, handed the reins to the caretaker at 7 a.m. and went home.'

'That's when someone could have stolen the mangoes—during the shift change,' thought Shyam.

'Next week, I will stay here and catch the thief myself,' he announced.

Shyam marked the mangoes on the special tree that were going to be ready the next week and went home.

Chapter Three

Six days later, Shyam came to the grove after finishing his dinner. He lit a lamp so he could keep an eye on his surroundings. While lighting it, he accidentally burnt his finger. Impatiently, he rubbed it. He did not want to sleep, and the burning pain on his finger did not allow him to sleep either. He regularly flashed the lamp at the mangoes hanging from the special tree.

BANG BANG BANG

At around 3 a.m. in the morning, he got the whiff of a beautiful fragrance—an aroma that he had never smelled before. It was enchanting. The night guard had been correct. Shyam, however, stayed focussed and decided not to follow the fascinating aroma. He took out cotton balls from his pocket and plugged them into his nose, so that the tempting aroma could not distract him. He sat on a chair, pretending to sleep. Suddenly, he heard loud banging.

He peeked through his eyelids, just a little, and saw a small door opening in the trunk of another old mango tree in the orchard. To his bewilderment, a pretty girl in a mango-coloured sari came out of the trunk. She looked like a porcelain doll, and she nimbly climbed up the tree that had the sweet mangoes. Soon, she plucked the ripe mangoes and was about to head back into the trunk when Shyam called out to her loudly and yelled, 'Stop! Thief!' She was taken aback. When she turned around, her eyes sparkled with curiosity.

'STOP! THIEF!'

'Who are you?' asked Shyam. 'Are you the thief who has been stealing my delicious and special mangoes?'

The girl laughed and her laughter sounded like the tinkling of delicate bells. 'I am not a thief, sir. I am just a hungry person,' she said.

'If you were hungry, you could have asked someone here for food. We would have given you some. We always take care of the people around us. Why did you decide to steal instead of asking for help?' Shyam asked, puzzled.

The girl sighed. She sat down below the tree and began her story. It went thus . . .

Chapter Four

Many years ago, my father owned this fruit orchard that now belongs to you. Due to the extraordinary charitable work of his ancestors, the god of mangoes blessed my father and the land, and gave him one mango seed. He said, 'Plant this mango seed. The tree will grow in no time and produce the sweetest mangoes you have ever eaten. One mango is enough to satisfy anyone's hunger.'

We did what he told us, and people began to flock to our orchard like bees. My father distributed one mango each, free of cost, to every hungry person who came to our orchard.

It occurred to me that we could sell those mangoes and make money, but my father refused to sell them. We sold other fruits, but we still weren't well off. My father always said, 'We are blessed that our mangoes taste like nectar. We can't give real nectar to people, but we can give these heavenly mangoes to them. So dear daughter, don't ever sell them—they are a gift from the god of mangoes himself.'

I disagreed. I thought my father was not thinking about our family's future. I thought selling the mangoes would solve all our money problems, yet Father always overruled me.

One day, when Father was out of town, I oversaw the harvesting of the mangoes. I collected all the mangoes but did not give them to anyone. A man in green clothes approached me and asked for the sweet mangoes.

Though Father would have given him a mango immediately, I refused. 'Pay money and take as many as you want,' I said. I wanted to earn some money from the mangoes and show Father how this could turn our family's fortune.

'But your father gives the mangoes to me for free,' the man said.

'Sir, I am not my father.'

'Please, young lady, give me two mangoes.'

I stayed silent.

He said, 'How about just one mango?'

I refused.

'But I am extremely hungry,' he insisted.

'I am sorry, sir, but I cannot help you.'

As I said those words, the man transformed into a magical being. With great authority, the magical being said, 'I am the god of mangoes. I like your father because he is generous and helps people who are hungry. Your father never sold mangoes from this blessed tree.

'When a person asks for a mango, it must be given to them. Even if a person asks out of greed, they cannot eat more than one. This is not the same as greed for gold, money and land, which never ends. Food is the only thing in this world that can satisfy your hunger fully. Today, you have not used your boon for the right purpose. You have driven out those who are hungry and needy. Here is your punishment—may you realize what it means to be hungry and may you be forced to steal food to fill your stomach.'

That is the moment when I realized my mistake and fell at his feet. I apologized for not knowing what hunger feels like and not caring enough for people in need.

The god of mangoes said, 'If you are really sorry, then the day someone catches you stealing, the curse will disappear. Until then, you can live in a small house inside the trunk of the mango tree and steal the fruit to survive.'

I agreed with him but I also had one request, 'I want to ask you for a favour.'

'Sorry, young girl, I don't think you are in a position to ask for anything.'

'Please, o god of mangoes,' I said. 'The mangoes are extremely delicious, and many people will fall into the trap of trying to make money out of them, just like I did. If all mangoes turned sweet and people planted and grew their own sweet mangoes, it would be a boon to humankind. May I request you to make all mangoes sweet and delicious after my curse ends?

'Perhaps in later times, the mango will be crowned the king of all fruits and there will be a new idiom—as delicious as mangoes!'

The god of mangoes smiled and replied, 'I like your suggestion. This shows that you are thinking about others. I will make most of the mangoes sweet but only the ones that grow during the summer season. Their magical sweetness will satisfy a person's hunger and quench their thirst on hot summer days. The sour ones can be used to make pickles or eaten as chutneys that will last throughout the year.

'Moreover, people could offer mangoes to gods in prayer or distribute them among friends and relatives. Such acts will be considered pious and generous.'

'What a fascinating story!' said Shyam.

'And that is how I came to live in this tree,' said the girl. 'But from today, I am free from the curse. Thank you for setting me free. From now on, everyone can get sweet mangoes in summer because of the magic of the god of mangoes.'

The girl smiled.

Shyam smiled back and said, 'What a blessing to us! I promise to share all the mangoes of my grove with everyone. Please stay. I would love to share them with you too.'

The girl shook her head. 'I can't stay. Besides, I ate these sweet mangoes every day. Too much greed is not a good thing. Family is important and I must go back to mine,' she added and began to walk away.

Shyam glanced at the trunk of the tree and saw that the little door had magically vanished.

The girl paced to the end of the grove and kept walking until Shyam could not see her any more.

Henceforth, all mangoes became sweet
in summer blessed by the magic bestowed
upon them by the god of mangoes.

Acknowledgements

Mango has been a traditional Indian fruit for a very long time. Its colour is enchanting, and its sweetness is par excellence. No wonder it is called the king of all fruits in India. There are hundreds of varieties of mangoes that grow at different times all over the country with varying flavour. I always wondered why mangoes taste so delicious and what magic nature has done on this fruit. This is how the story came to me. Please share this wonderful fruit with your loved ones and multiply the joy.

I would like to thank Shrutkeerti Khurana, my trusted editor, for her work on this book. I would also like to thank Sohini Mitra, my publisher from Penguin Random House, the editorial team at Penguin Random House and the illustrator Priyanka Pachpande for her enchanting artworks.

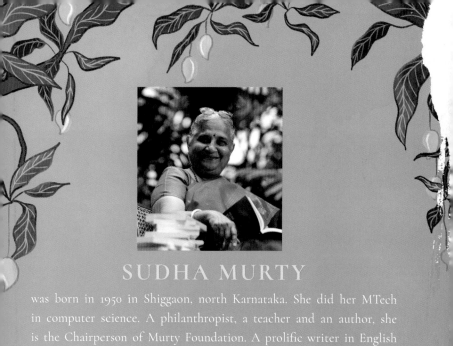

SUDHA MURTY

was born in 1950 in Shiggaon, north Karnataka. She did her MTech in computer science. A philanthropist, a teacher and an author, she is the Chairperson of Murty Foundation. A prolific writer in English and Kannada, she has penned novels, technical books, travelogues, collections of short stories and non-fiction pieces, and bestselling books for children. Her books have been translated into all major Indian languages. Sudha Murty is the recipient of the R K Narayan Award for Literature (2006), The Padma Shri (2006), the Attimabbe Award from the Government of Karnataka for excellence in Kannada Literature (2011) and the Lifetime Achievement Award at the 2018 Crossword Book awards. She weaves magical tales and especially enjoys writing for young readers. A generation of children has grown up reading her books, and her stories have been included in textbooks across schools in India.

Dear Reader

May your life be as bright,
as the colour of mangoes

With affection

Murty

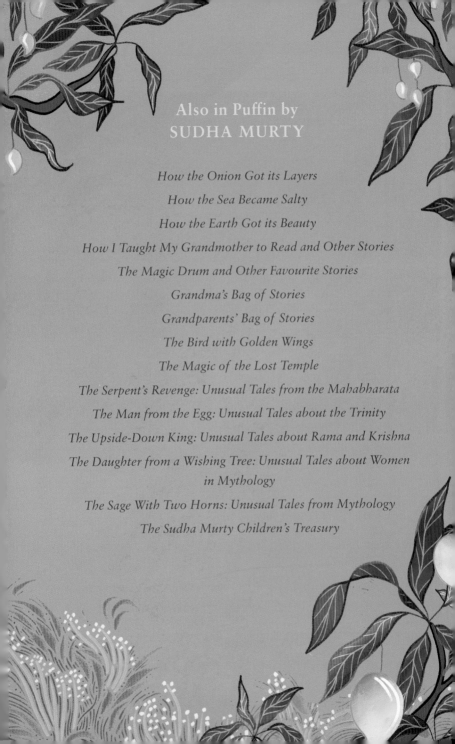

Also in Puffin by
SUDHA MURTY

SHRUTKEERTI KHURANA

(or Shrutee) is an independent editor of several fiction, non-fiction and children's books, and also the Program Director at Infosys Foundation. She holds a Master's degree in Business Administration and a Bachelor's Degree in Engineering. Shrutee lives in Bangalore with her family and three dogs. Her work can be found at www.shrutee.in.

PRIYANKA PACHPANDE

is an illustrator and visual artist, currently based out of Pune. She enjoys playing with colours and exploring moods in her illustrations. Her illustrations transport you to dreamy worlds full of magic. Crayons, ink, watercolour and Procreate on the iPad are some of her favourite mediums. Priyanka also loves to travel and is a foodie at heart. Her work can be found at www.priyankapachpande.com.